The Adventures of
SAMMY
THE SKUNK
BOOK I

WRITTEN BY ADELE A. ROBERTS

ILLUSTRATED BY KATHY HOLLAND

WestBow Press books may be ordered through booksellers or by contacting:

WestBow Press
A Division of Thomas Nelson & Zondervan
1663 Liberty Drive
Bloomington, IN 47403
www.westbowpress.com
1 (866) 928-1240

ISBN: 978-1-4908-8164-5 (sc)
ISBN: 978-1-5127-0825-7 (e)

Print information available on the last page.

WestBow Press rev. date: 8/24/2015

WESTBOW
PRESS®
A DIVISION OF THOMAS NELSON
& ZONDERVAN

CONTENTS

"And God saw every thing that he had made, and behold, it was very good." Genesis 1:31 (KJV)

CHAPTER ONE

The deep woods was a perfect place for the forest animals to live. The trees were tall for climbing, the bushes were bushy for hiding, the overgrown grasses and wild berries were good for eating, the dead branches and dried leaves were used for making homes, and the lake and river were good places for the animals to play or get water to drink.

The main entrance was a path that was guarded by Mr. and Mrs. Owl, who loved the forest animals and were watching day and night to make sure no danger would come to them. They greeted new animals and asked why they had come to the woods. Then the owls explained the ways of the deep woods.

One day a handsome animal with beautiful light brown and red fur pranced into the deep woods. His tail was like a plume. It waved as he walked, and the fur on it was so long it almost touched the ground. He was quite a magnificent-looking fox.

When Mr. Fox entered the deep woods he was greeted by the owls, but he never talked to them. He nodded his head and quickly ran down the path where he disappeared into the woods.

It wasn't long after Mr. Fox entered the deep woods when Miss Deer saw him breaking one of the rules of the woods. He was seen running after the other animals and frightening them. Mr. and Mrs. Owl did not have a chance to tell Mr. Fox the rule about chasing in the woods. *The only time an animal could chase another was when they were playing "tag."* Now the animals wondered, "Was Mr. Fox playing with them, or was he hunting them?"

It was on a beautiful sunny day when a little skunk named Sammy entered the deep woods quite by accident.

Sammy and his mother and father lived in a little home outside of the deep woods. He went to school. He went shopping with his mother and dad. He had rules to live by. He had chores to do. He slept in a soft bed.

Sometimes he would look at the deep woods and wonder if there were skunks like him. No one that he knew ever went into the deep woods, and his mother and father told Sammy to keep away from it. Sammy wondered why, but did as his mother and father told him.

Sammy was playing outside one afternoon when a group of older animals, bigger and stronger, made fun of him because he was so small. They said he was never going to amount to anything and he would never do anything important in life. They ran after him and chased him to the edge of the deep woods.

"Oh, poor little Sammy," they laughed. "Don't go into the deep woods! A little ant may eat you up!" They ran away and left Sammy standing by himself. He felt very hurt. Big tears began to roll down his cheeks.

"Why do they make fun of me? I know I'm small. Maybe they're right. Maybe I will never amount to anything." He looked at the path leading into the deep woods. He took a few steps in, sat down, and put his hands over his head.

From the deep woods came a voice. "Who-o-o? Who-o-o?"
Sammy turned his head one way and then another. He wondered who was asking him his name.

Who do you think was asking Sammy his name?

CHAPTER TWO

"Sammy. My name is Sammy," he replied.

"Who-o-o? Who-o-o?" came the question again.

This time Sammy said a little louder, "I'm Sammy! I'm Sammy the skunk!"

Sammy looked up and saw two owls sitting in a tree, looking down at him.

Mr. Owl began questioning Sammy. "Can you tell us why you are here? Are you a runaway? We have many animals that come into the deep woods to get away from something. If you have a problem, we could help you. We're very wise, you know."

Sammy stopped crying and wiped his tears from his face. "My friends make fun of me because I'm so—" Before Sammy could say another word, he heard a thundering noise. It was so loud he couldn't hear the owls telling him to **hide!** The animals of the deep woods were hurrying to get away from something.

"Run! Run! Get out of the way! Oh, this is terrible! This is awful! I have no time to stop and talk! Mr. Fox is running after us! He's coming!" cried Miss Deer.

Miss Deer pranced past Sammy and shouted, "Oh dear! Oh dear! That is all I have to say! Oh dear! I must go fast! Mr. Fox is after ME!" She glanced back at Sammy, who didn't know what to do or where to run. "Follow me! Follow me!" she cried. Instead Sammy stepped behind a tree so the other animals wouldn't run over him. Then he did something very brave.

He peered into the woods and saw a sleek-looking animal coming toward him. Sammy stepped out from behind the tree and didn't move. The fox stopped and smiled. He leaned down and whispered in the ear of Sammy, "My, but you're little." Mr. Fox laughed out loud and started running after the other animals.

Sammy wasn't very happy about what Mr. Fox said to him. He had heard those words too many times before. He called to Mr. Fox. "Mr. Fox, oh, Mr. Fox, I have something for you." Mr. Fox stopped and looked around at Sammy. Sammy stood firm and glared back at him. What could this little skunk have for him? Mr. Fox didn't feel he was in any danger, so he began to walk back to Sammy.

What do you think Sammy was going to give Mr. Fox?

CHAPTER THREE

Sammy stood like a statue waiting for him. As soon as Mr. Fox was in front of him, Sammy sprayed Mr. Fox with everything he had! Mr. Fox yelped and turned around in circles before he took off down the path. Sammy started to laugh as he saw Mr. Fox running away. He shouted, "Mr. Fox, you'll never be able to sneak up on any of the animals in the deep woods again! They'll smell you before you can get close to them!"

The forest animals were watching from a distance and now began to come out to see who this very brave animal was. Miss Deer was the first to speak. "You weren't afraid of Mr. Fox! What is your name? We have never seen you in the deep woods before."

"My name is Sammy," he replied.

Miss Deer bent her head down, and Sammy began to back away. She was very big compared to him, and for a moment he was afraid. Miss Deer sensed he was scared and lovingly said, "Oh, don't be afraid, Sammy. We want to thank you. Have you come to live with us? We'd love to have you."

"No, not exactly," said Sammy. He hung his head and began to tell them what happened.

"I was chased to the edge of the deep woods by some friends who said some bad things about me." He paused for a moment and, with a slight smile, raised his head and said, "I believe I'm already beginning to feel better! I know I'm small, and maybe I'll hear hurtful words again, but today I actually did something to help all of you."

"Sammy, real friends don't make you feel bad," said Miss Deer. "If you spend some time with us, we'll show you what true friends are really like. Stay with us today and I'll introduce you to the other forest animals."

Mr. and Mrs. Owl smiled as they saw how the animals surrounded Sammy and showed their appreciation and acceptance of this little skunk.

Throughout the day the animals introduced themselves and took Sammy to their homes. They showed him all the fun places in the deep woods.

Every once in a while, when the animals were running and playing, they would smell a skunk and think they saw Mr. Fox watching from a distance.

Sammy wondered what Mr. Fox was thinking and feeling. Did he do the right thing by spraying Mr. Fox? Did that hurt Mr. Fox's feelings just as much as words had hurt his?

How do you think Mr. Fox was feeling?

CHAPTER FOUR

It was getting darker outside, and it was time for Sammy to leave the deep woods. As he bid farewell to Mr. Owl and Mrs. Owl, Sammy listened to their encouraging words.

"Sammy, you may be small, but you used what you had today to help others. You are very brave. I'm sure Mr. Fox isn't happy about what happened to him, but I think you taught him a lesson. He'll never run after the forest animals again, and we'll always know where he is."

Sammy was happy to have new friends. The animals followed him to the edge of the deep woods, and he turned and waved at them as he walked home.

Sammy's mother and father were waiting for him. "Where have you been?" asked Mr. Skunk. Your mother and I were worried about you.

Sammy told them about the fox and how he had helped the forest animals. "The deep woods is a wonderful place! I found many friends. Do you think I can go back again?" he asked.

Sammy's mother and father nodded their heads yes, but warned him to be very careful.

As he lay in bed that evening he thought about Mr. Fox. He knew that someday soon he would go back to the deep woods. He wanted to visit his new friends, but he also wanted to see Mr. Fox. He fell asleep thinking about what he would say to him.

Do you think Sammy will ever see Mr. Fox again?

LIFE LESSON | FORGIVENESS

Question:

Have you ever said something to someone that hurt their feelings?
What should you do if you did?

Scripture:

"And be ye kind one to another, tenderhearted, forgiving one another" Ephesians 4:32a (KJV)

Truth about God

God is always kind and forgiving.

Lesson:

God made you different from everyone else. It is wonderful to know God loves you just as you are. Does He know how you are feeling right now? Yes! God knows everything about you.

CHAPTER ONE

Sammy had become well known by the animals in the deep forest. He had sprayed Mr. Fox as only a skunk can do, and the fox stayed away from the other animals and the animals stayed away from him. Once in a while they would see Mr. Fox in the river washing, and the animals would grin and walk away.

Sammy thought about Mr. Fox often. It was true that all the forest animals knew just where Mr. Fox was at all times, but they also deliberately stayed away from him. They laughed at Mr. Fox from a distance. Sammy knew how it felt to be made fun of. He certainly didn't like it, and he wondered what he could do to help Mr. Fox.

One day Sammy went to visit Mr. and Mrs. Owl to discuss Mr. Fox. He wanted to know if they had seen him and how he was doing. Under his arm Sammy carried a can of tomato juice. Sammy knew if Mr. Fox could wash himself with tomato juice it would take the skunk smell away.

As he entered the deep woods, Mr. and Mrs. Owl were not in the tree. It was unusually quiet and Sammy began to be concerned.

"Is anyone here?" he asked. He started walking deeper into the woods, hoping to find someone.

"Hello, your friend Sammy is here," he called, but nobody answered.

He had gone only a short distance when he saw Miss Deer. She seemed very confused and was talking to herself.

"Let's see, it's down this path for a little ways. Then I must turn and take another path, and then I come to the bend and turn either left or right. Oh, this is terrible. It is awful. I'm lost in my own woods!" She began to cry. "I don't know where the surprise party is going to be."

Just then she looked up and saw Sammy. "Oh, Sammy, how nice of you to come to the surprise party. The surprise party is for everyone, but I haven't the slightest idea where everyone is! Can you help, Sammy?"

Do you think that Sammy can help Miss Deer?

CHAPTER TWO

"I'll tell you what we'll do," said Sammy. "Let's sit down for a moment, and then we'll decide which way we should go."

As they sat quietly and Miss Deer thought once more about the directions that were given to her, they heard a rustling sound coming through the bushes.

"Sh-h-h," whispered Sammy. "Someone is coming and I believe I smell a skunk!"

Sammy and Miss Deer looked into the woods and saw Mr. Fox sniffing the ground to get the scent of the forest animals. Mr. Fox knew they had all gone together somewhere, and he wanted to know where they were and what they were doing.

Mr. Fox walked through the woods, turning one way and then another. Miss Deer and Sammy followed behind, walking very quietly. It wasn't long before they heard a joyful sound of animals laughing and singing. It was very loud and the forest animals didn't smell or hear Mr. Fox creeping closer and closer.

Sammy didn't know what Mr. Fox had in mind. Was it a free dinner? Sammy thought the animals were in danger, so he ran ahead of Mr. Fox and yelled as loud as he could, "Mr. Fox is coming!"

The sound of shouting from Sammy scared Mr. Fox, and he ran into the woods.

The animals stopped what they were doing. They looked into the woods and saw Mr. Fox sitting with his paws over his eyes. He was crying very loudly and the tears were streaming down his face.

The animals heard Mr. Fox say, "All I wanted to do was see what all of you were doing. I wasn't going to hurt anyone. I smell so bad that I haven't been around anyone in a long, long time."

Mr. Owl flew in a tree over where Mr. Fox was sitting and looked down at him. "Mr. Fox, you have been scaring the animals by running after them. They didn't know if you wanted to be a friend and play with them or if you wanted to hurt them!"

Mr. Fox looked up to Mr. Owl and apologized. "I'm so sorry. You were having such a fun time before I came. I am so ashamed for scaring everyone. Please forgive me."

Do you think the animals will forgive Mr. Fox?

CHAPTER THREE

Mr. Owl didn't say a word. The animals were waiting to see what he was going to do.

Mr. Owl looked at Mrs. Owl, and Mrs. Owl laughingly said, "Mr. Fox, come join the party! We **want** you to be our friend! Today we are celebrating our lives in the deep woods and how lucky we are to have good friends that care about one another. Our surprise party is for everyone, and now that includes YOU!"

Together the animals shouted, "Come on, Mr. Fox! We're happy you are here!"

Mr. Fox wiped the tears from his face and walked toward them. But as he came nearer, the animals backed away and held their noses.

Sammy smiled. He felt good to know the animals were ready to forgive Mr. Fox, but he said, "Mr. Fox, you **really** stink! I brought something with me today to wash away the smell."

Sammy held up a can of tomato juice.

"Mr. Fox, you walk in front of us and head for the river. We'll line up and follow you. Once you see the water, jump in," instructed Sammy.

Mr. Fox proudly led the way, with his beautiful tail waving in the wind. The animals made a line behind him, holding their noses.

Once they got to the river, everyone jumped in. Sammy opened the tomato juice and poured the juice all over Mr. Fox. Mr. Fox sat very still, and the animals saw a big smile on his face as the tomato juice dripped over his beautiful fur.

Do you think the tomato juice will take the skunk smell off the fur of Mr. Fox?

CHAPTER FOUR

Mr. Fox was so happy to be accepted and to get rid of the skunk smell! He joined the animals at the party and they played games, sang, and ate. Of course, the one who had the most fun of all was Mr. Fox.

When it was time to leave, Mr. Fox looked at Sammy and thanked him. "Can we be friends?" he asked.

"Of course, you **are** my friend!" replied Sammy.

Mr. Fox continued, "Sammy, I am so grateful that you and the forest animals like me. It wasn't fun being alone all the time."

Mr. and Mrs. Owl looked down from their home in the tree and said, "I believe someone learned today that in order to have friends one must be a friend."

Mr. Fox seemed very happy as he walked with Sammy to the edge of the deep woods.

"Sammy," said Mr. Fox, "if I want to see you again, I'll stand at the edge of the deep woods and shake my tail. That will be my special sign to you. Okay?"

Sammy thought that was a very good idea. Sammy waved good-bye and looked back at him. He had a feeling that their friendship, although just beginning, was going to last a long time.

That night when Sammy lay in bed, he wondered what the animals were doing. "Had they all gone to bed? Were they thinking about what they would do tomorrow?"

Sammy knew he would go into the deep woods again. He fell asleep with a smile on his face. It had been another good day in the deep woods with his forest friends. He really did like Mr. Fox.

LIFE LESSON | A TRUE FRIEND

Question:

Have you ever ignored someone because you thought they didn't like you?
How do you become a friend?

Scripture:

"A friend loveth at all times" Proverbs 17:17a (KJV)

Truth about God:

God is always faithful and loving even when we are not.

Lesson:

Did you know that God sees everything you do? You can't hide from Him. He sees how you treat others and what you are thinking about them. God wants you to love and care for others as He loves and cares for you.

CHAPTER ONE

"Oh, it's terrible! It's simply awful! Oh, it's so terrible! What can we do?"

Miss Deer was very upset as she ran down the path to see Mr. and Mrs. Owl. She looked up at them and said again, "Oh, it's terrible. Just terrible! That is all I have to say." She was prancing around in a circle, saying the same thing over and over.

The owls looked down at her and became very concerned. "Miss Deer, settle down. Stop circling beneath us. You're making us dizzy just watching you. Soon we may fall out of the tree! Can you stop and tell us what is just so terrible and awful?" Mr. Owl asked.

Still very flustered and nervous, Miss Deer began:

"Well, I was going down to the river to see the Beaver family. You know they had some more children, and I was on my way to give Mrs. Beaver a present. That is when I heard Mr. Beaver calling Mrs. Beaver. She came running from the woods and I joined her. Together we ran to the river to see what had happened. Mr. Beaver was sitting on a log and he looked okay. He didn't say anything for a while. He was staring at the river where he was building his new home for his family. He had begun a strong dam, and his home WAS going to be absolutely beautiful, BUT—"

"What do you mean, WAS?" asked Mr. Owl.

"Well," continued Miss Deer, "it is so terrible! Just awful! When Mr. Beaver opened his mouth to speak, we saw he had lost all of his chewing teeth! Two of his upper and two of his lower teeth were gone! Mrs. Beaver and I tried to find them, to put them back in—"

Mrs. Owl interrupted, "Miss Deer, that is silly! You can't put teeth back once they have come out! But, out of curiosity, did you find them?"

"We did! We did!" Miss Deer pranced around as if she was happy. "Do you want to see them?" she asked the owls.

"No, no, no! Tell us. Where are they?" asked Mr. Owl.

Where do you think Mr. Beaver's teeth could be?

CHAPTER TWO

"They're stuck in an oak tree! Mr. Beaver bit into that hard tree and his teeth snapped right off, and there they are for everyone to see. I must go now and tell our friends about this terrible thing," said Miss Deer.

The owls looked at each other, and Mrs. Owl said, "What do you think we can do to help?"

"Now don't rush me. I must give this considerable thought," answered Mr. Owl. "Mr. Beaver does have a problem. If he can't chew down those trees, he won't have a home for his family this winter. We must do something, but what?"

"Perhaps we could find someone to chew for him!" said Mrs. Owl very sweetly.

"That is impossible! Only a beaver can do what a beaver does," replied Mr. Owl.

The two owls sat in the tree, thinking as hard as they could. What could they do to help?

It wasn't long before almost all the other animals of the woods heard about Mr. Beaver's teeth stuck in the oak tree. They went down to console Mr. Beaver. With their heads bowed, no one saying a word, they sat and wondered what they could do.

When Mr. Fox heard about Mr. Beaver losing his teeth, he went to the Beaver home and saw the forest animals sitting in a circle with sad faces. Mr. and Mrs. Beaver were with them. Mr. Beaver had his mouth closed and didn't want to say anything.

Mr. Fox said, "I have an idea! I know what to do!"

The animals looked up and stared at him. Waiting to hear what he was going to say, they leaned toward him in silence.

What idea do you think Mr. Fox had?

21

CHAPTER THREE

"I'm going to get Sammy! He has helped us before and maybe he will know what to do again."

Together the animals said, "I think he is right! Sammy will know what to do! Let's go find him."

They jumped up and were ready to go on a hunt for Sammy.

"Wait," said Mr. Fox. "Let me. I know how to get him quickly. He and I have agreed that if I do need him, I would stand at the edge of the deep woods and shake my tail. It is a flag that says, 'Help!'"

Sammy had just finished eating when he looked out the window and saw the waving of a big tail. "It's Mr. Fox!" he explained to his mother and father. "I must go now! Something is wrong and my friends need me." He opened the door and ran as fast as he could to the deep woods.

He was in such a hurry that as he came nearer to Mr. Fox, he couldn't stop running and he ran right into him. They both fell over and Sammy landed on top of him.

Sammy was out of breath and panting, but he managed to say in between breaths, "Well, here I am! Do you need something?"

A little shocked and a little out of breath himself, Mr. Fox said, "Let's get up first, and then I'll tell you what has happened." Mr. Fox brushed himself off and stood up.

"Sammy, Mr. Beaver lost his chewing teeth. He needs to make a home for his family, and he can't make a home because he doesn't have his front teeth!"

Sammy listened, and after he thought for a while, he asked Mr. Fox a question.

"I met Dr. Raccoon when I was in the deep woods. Did you know he is a dentist? He has a very nice office in a big old stump. I would recommend that we visit him and tell him about Mr. Beaver. If anyone can help, it would be Dr. Raccoon."

Sammy and Mr. Fox began their journey deep in the woods and soon came to Dr. Raccoon's office. On the door was a sign with large bold letters that read, **"Need a smile on your face? You're at the right place."**

Do you think Dr. Raccoon can help Mr. Beaver?

CHAPTER FOUR

Sammy knocked on the door, and soon Dr. Raccoon stood in front of them, looking very professional in his white jacket.

Acting a little surprised and talking very fast, Dr. Raccoon said, "You're right on time! Sit down and I'll start immediately! Who wants to go first? What hurts? Do you want me to pull a tooth? What are you here for?" Then he became very quiet, stopped asking questions, and stared at them.

"We're here to ask you a question," said Sammy.

"Well, if you need to ask me something, do it very quickly, for I have many patients waiting," replied Dr. Raccoon.

Sammy and Mr. Fox looked around and saw no one in the waiting room. Mr. Fox shrugged his shoulders as if saying, "I don't understand."

Sammy told him about Mr. Beaver. When Sammy finished, Dr. Raccoon got up without saying a word. He went into another room and came back with a set of false teeth. Dr. Raccoon had made four big white teeth for cutting down trees.

Sammy was very surprised. "How did you know?"

"Miss Deer told me. I began working on new teeth for Mr. Beaver as soon as I heard about his accident. I was waiting for someone to show up at my office so I could give them the new teeth. I would have taken them to Mr. Beaver myself, but as you can see, I am so terribly busy with all my patients that I couldn't leave the office," remarked Dr. Raccoon.

Sammy thanked Dr. Raccoon and told him what a wonderful thing he had done for the Beaver family. He also told Dr. Raccoon that if he knew of any forest animals that needed a dentist, he would send them directly to him.

Dr. Raccoon shook paws with Sammy and Mr. Fox as they left his office. Before they were totally out of sight, Dr. Raccoon shouted, "Are you sure you don't want a tooth pulled, or maybe Mr. Fox you'd like your teeth sharpened?"

They both politely shook their heads. "No, but it was very kind of you to ask. Perhaps some other time we will need some dental work done. I'm sure we'll see each other again."

Do you think Mr. Beaver will like his new teeth?

CHAPTER FIVE

On the way to Mr. Beaver's house, Sammy told Mr. Fox that it was strange that not one of the other animals remembered Dr. Raccoon. Maybe they didn't want to believe that someday they may need a dentist.

The animals were waiting for Sammy and Mr. Fox. They wondered if Sammy had a solution for Mr. Beaver's problem.

Sammy stood in front of Mr. Beaver and with a smile on his face held out the new set of teeth. All the animals began to clap and cheer.

They watched as Mrs. Beaver put the special glue on them and placed them in Mr. Beaver's mouth. "There dear. Now you go out there and chew again! We'll go with you to the river to see if they work!"

The animals lined up and walked with Mr. Beaver to the river. They were quiet as they watched Mr. Beaver take his first chew.

Mr. Beaver looked up and smiled. He gnawed right through the first log and began on the second. He was so happy that he didn't want to stop!

Mrs. Beaver gave him a bit of advice. "Now remember, dear, don't go chewing on those hard oak trees."

Mr. Beaver looked up just long enough to smile at her. He kept on gnawing. He was anxious to finish their home.

The animals shouted, "They work! Those teeth really work! Where did you get them, Sammy?"

Sammy explained that he and Mr. Fox went to visit Dr. Raccoon, the dentist. Out of the kindness of Dr. Raccoon's heart he made a set of teeth for Mr. Beaver.

Miss Deer gently nudged Sammy with her velvet nose, looked at him with her huge brown eyes, and said, "You have helped us out again. I know you don't live in the deep woods, but we consider you part of our family." She leaned down and gave Sammy a kiss on his nose.

Mr. Fox walked Sammy to the edge of the deep forest and bid him farewell. He watched him until he could no longer see Sammy. He was so happy that Sammy was his friend.

When Sammy went to bed that night he lay awake for a while, wondering about all his friends in the deep woods. He knew they would call upon him again. He was wondering what would happen next.

LIFE LESSON | SERVING OTHERS

Question:

How can you show kindness to one another?

Scripture:

"By love serve one another." Galatians 5:13b (KJV)

Truth about God:

Even though Jesus is God, He became a servant and helped others.

Discuss:

God is pleased when those who know Jesus show kindness to others. God wants you to be an example of Him through the way you speak and act. Just as Jesus served us by coming to this world to live and die for us, we need to give of ourselves to help others.

CPSIA information can be obtained
at www.ICGtesting.com
Printed in the USA
LVHW07n1953180618
581156LV00003B/5/P